A Tyr....

I hope you enjoy the book

ISBN: 978-1-9165009-0-7

For my three scamps

Contents

A lot of words and a handful of pictures

Based on a true story

Eddie and Bolan

Eddie was an ordinary ten year old boy. He lived on an ordinary street, in an ordinary red-brick semi with his ordinary family. He had ordinary chestnut brown hair that was cut in an ordinary style. He wore ordinary clothes, attended an ordinary school and despite his Mum regularly telling him how wonderful he was, he was actually fairly ordinary at most things. In fact, if you looked up ordinary in the dictionary it wouldn't come as a huge surprise to find a portrait of Eddie there looking back at you, for he was as ordinary as they come. However, he was an ordinary boy with an extra-ordinary friend!

Eddie's amazing discovery was made on one of the foraging walks that he often took to Black

Gateaux Forest. The dense forest was one of the largest in the world and there was always a plentiful supply of bugs and creepy crawlies to be found there, which Eddie liked to use to spice up his sister Lainey's food. Despite being warned many times to stay at the edge of forest, Eddie would often venture further than he should to find the juiciest specimens. And that's when he found it!

Too big to belong to a bird, Eddie had brought the egg home, somewhat out of curiosity but mostly because he knew that adding it to the class nature table would boost his chances of being star of the week. Not that Eddie cared about pleasing his teacher, mind you. He just wanted one of Miss Taiken's fabulous prizes, or good behaviour bribes as his Dad called them, the same as everyone else. So far this year Eddie had been overlooked each Friday afternoon, as his efforts in school were C grade (at best!) but Eddie felt sure that bringing in a weird and wonderful egg would make up for all that. However, little did Eddie know at the time that the egg was never destined to reach the nature table and that bringing it home would turn his life completely upside down!

Bolan had hatched on a Sunday night. Eddie had returned to his bedroom, after his fortnightly bath, to discover him sitting there proudly on the cluttered desk his parents had bought him, in the hope that his homework would be completed on a more regular basis. Like most boys, Eddie had gone through a dinosaur phase a few years ago, so he was pretty sure he knew what he was looking at. Only, he couldn't believe what he was looking at, as what he was looking at was something nobody had ever looked at. Not in real life anyway. What he was looking at, was a baby T-rex!

Bolan was named after Marc Bolan from the band T. Rex, a group of long haired hippie types that his Nan, and other old fogies, rocked out to back in ancient times. Eddie had toyed around with a few other names, like T- bone, Cruncher and Sherlock Bones, but he stuck with Bolan because of his Nan. His Nan loved Marc Bolan and Eddie loved his Nan, so that was that! Eddie always wanted a pet of his own and now he had one that no one else had. Bolan was even better than the California kingsnake his neighbour Bill Ding had that ate whole mice.

It wasn't all peaches and cream though. At first, Eddie found caring for Bolan tough going. As anyone who has a pet will tell you, it's a full time job and that's if you have a normal pet like a goldfish, let alone a baby T-rex that had to be kept hidden in a small bedroom all day! Eddie's parents weren't keen on having a pet and he knew that if anyone discovered that an animal thought to have died out sixty-five million years ago was living in his bedroom, it would cause a hullaballoo to say the least. The only person Eddie ever told Bolan about was his best friend,

Justin Time. Eddie trusted Justin completely. After all, he had kept the biggest secret Eddie ever had....that he had a girlfriend! Eddie had been crazy about Hazel Nutt and he would go round to her house every day after school and for large chunks of the weekend, but that all stopped when Eddie dumped Hazel out of the blue, coincidently around the same time her brother's virtual reality headset broke.

After a while, Eddie and Bolan found a routine that suited them well.

Before he left for school in the morning, Eddie would put on a film, like Land before Time, Jurassic park or Night at the Museum....anything that had dinosaurs in it really. Bolan loved the films. He especially liked the scene in Jurassic Park where the guy gets eaten while he's sitting on the toilet. Eddie was sure that Bolan smirked every time he watched it. This did worry Eddie a little though, as it wasn't unusual for his Dad to leave the bathroom door open while he was in there. Many times, Eddie had walked along the narrow upstairs landing and found his Dad squatted on the toilet reading one of his soccer magazines. If Bolan was to escape from his bedroom and see him sat there, who knows what would happen?

When school was over, Eddie would rush home and give Bolan the leftovers from his packed lunch and then raid the cupboards for things that he would like for dinner. Eddie mostly fed Bolan ham, chicken and beef because he knew that T-rex's are carnivores. What Eddie was surprised to discover though, is that Bolan's favourite food was actually baked beans! Bolan loved them and could eat tins and tins each and every day. The only problem with this was what came after. As Eddie soon found out, there is no smell in this world as putrid as a dinosaur fart. After a dinner of beans, Eddie's room would stink. Actually, to say it would stink wouldn't do it justice at all. It was more of a stench. A stench is worse than a stink. A stink smells rotten but it passes, given time. However, a stench is so horrid that it clings onto nearby objects, so that they still honk even after the original smell has vanished. Have you ever been to someone's house before and smelled fish, even though it was cooked days before? You probably have, because most fish give off a stench. Bolan's trumps were also definitely in the stench category. In fact they were so hideous, that Eddie was convinced that the whole theory about an asteroid colliding into the Earth causing the extinction of the dinosaurs was nonsense. He believed that they probably all just died out from choking on the toxic methane gas that was exhausted from their backsides!

After dinner, when night fell and his parents were downstairs in their pyjamas watching some dreary soap, Eddie and Bolan would sneak out. It was only a short drop from Eddie's bedroom window onto the conservatory roof. The pair would then leap down onto the trampoline in the back yard, bounce off and head out onto the street. Bolan was a lot like a dog. He got excited when his master came home, he enjoyed food and he loved going for walkies. Bolan loved being out in the fresh air, sniffing things and getting exercise, and usually he was as well behaved as any other dog. Eddie often felt bad that he couldn't take Bolan out more and walk him during the day, but it just wasn't possible. The image of a T-rex that you have seen in books and on T.V is fairly accurate, the only difference being that Bolan had soft downy fur, like that of a duckling, running along his spine. So, during the day he just wouldn't have passed for a dog, but during the twilight hours he could just about get away it.

"His Mother was a Rottweiler and his Father was a Peruvian Hairless," is what Eddie would say when other dog walkers stopped to ask him about the breed of his unusual looking 'dog'.

At bedtime, Eddie would brush Bolan's pearly whites….well actually, grubby yellows would be a better description, and then Bolan would go into Eddie's wardrobe, curl up in a blanket and sleep soundly all night.

Having Bolan as a pet was brilliant. It was the happiest Eddie had ever been. For instance, the past Halloween was the best ever. While Eddie's Frankenstein outfit and Justin's zombie attire were pretty shoddy, the neighbours were so amazed by the fantastic dinosaur 'costume' that their friend was wearing, they gave them more treats than they could carry. The three of them ate until they could barely move. Justin actually scoffed so many that he got sick, which spoiled the night a bit for him, but not for Bolan. He seemed to enjoy barf with half-digested gummi bear pieces nearly as much as baked beans.

Yes, Eddie's life was sweet for a while, but then, nothing lasts forever.

The Poodle and the Poo

No sooner had Eddie shut the sticky front door behind him, when he heard a thunderous roar from upstairs.

"Where the heck is he? Did you have the window open up here Lorraine?" Eddie's dad hollered down the stairs to his wife.

"It's January and it's minus one outside, why would I have the window open?" came the abrupt reply.

Eddie's Dad stormed down the stairs, pounding each step furiously with his clumpy shoes. Dad's stomp could be heard when his beloved Brighton and Hove Albion lost an important game, or when he had tried, and failed, to correctly assemble some simple flat pack furniture. 'The stomp of doom' Eddie called it and it was a warning to everyone in the family to stay out of Dad's way!

"Well where is he then? He can't have vanished into thin air. He must have escaped somehow!"

Instantly, Eddie cottoned on to what Dad was looking for. Lainey had asked for a puppy each and every year for her birthday. She wanted one so badly that she had a list of names ready, should she ever be allowed one. Hairy Pawter, Mr Wagglesworth and Mary Puppins were the best picks from the ghastly bunch of names that made up her top ten. Although she wanted a puppy so desperately, each and every year the answer was always the same. However, next week Lainey was to become a teenager and Mum and Dad believed that getting her a dog would teach her some responsibility, so they had bought her the poodle she so desired. Dad had collected the pup from a local breeder two days ago and it had been living in their bedroom until Lainey's big day.

"Where are you boy? Come out and I'll give you a treat," offered Eddie's Dad, as he bent down to look under the sofa. He groaned as he rose to his feet. Eddie's Dad was a short, stocky man. His box-like head sat on his neckless body, which made him look more like a Lego figurine than a human being. Suddenly, and without warning, Eddie's Dad swung around and turned his attention towards his son. "Have you got any idea where the pup has got to?" he asked accusingly, as his rectangular face loomed inches away from Eddie's.

"No Dad, I have no idea where he is."

Eddie's Dad fixed his steely stare on Eddie. He then squinted so hard that it looked like his eyeballs had been sucked into his face.

"Are you sure? I'll know if you're lying."

That was a lie in itself. Eddie's Dad never knew when he was lying. Keeping a young T-rex a secret wasn't easy and it required telling a regular stream of lies to cover up the strange and unusual incidents that often cropped up. So many in fact, that Eddie had become rather good at it.

"Oh leave him alone Tom, he's just got in the door. The puppy will be around here somewhere. He has to be," said Eddie's Mum, trying to reassure her husband.

Eddie knew it would be wise to get out of the way while the search was on. His Dad was a bubbling volcano and the longer he went without finding the poodle, the closer and closer he would come to erupting.

"I'm just going upstairs to do my homework," Eddie chirped, grabbing his satchel. Eddie's Dad turned sharply to look at him. Probably not the greatest excuse to escape, Eddie thought to himself, as usually his homework was completed minutes before leaving for school in the morning, if done at all! As Eddie climbed the stairs, he could feel his Dad's eyes crawling all over him and even though he knew nothing about the poodle, he now felt as if he had made himself the number one suspect in the case of the mysterious disappearing dog.

Once he reached the landing, Eddie quickly entered his bedroom and closed the door behind him.

"Come on Bolan, time for a pre-dinner snack," Eddie said, emptying the contents of his lunchbox onto the bed. It used to be that scraps were enough for Bolan. Some sandwich crusts, half a pear and a few raisins would satisfy him until dinner time. However now, Eddie didn't even bother opening his lunchbox during the school day, as Bolan would demolish the whole lot when he got home and still look for more.

"Bolan, where are you boy?"

Eddie scanned his bedroom. Bolan was nowhere to be seen but a banging coming from the wardrobe alerted Eddie to his presence. Eddie walked over and turned the handle of his closet, as it rattled sharply from left to right. "Bolan what are you doing in there?" he said, swinging open the wardrobe door.

Bolan looked up at Eddie. The white fluff nestled in his toothy grin stood out a mile against his mustard yellow fangs and deep green leathery hide.

"Why have you got cotton wool all over your mouth? Don't tell me you have been at Lainey's teddies again, you scamp." But as Eddie stared closer, he realised that it wasn't cotton wool at all. "No....you haven't?" cried Eddie. But he most certainly had.

"Bolan, you cannot do that. You naughty dinosaur!" Eddie said sternly, waggling his outstretched finger in Bolan's face. "That was Lainey's new pet!"

Bolan hung his oversized head and stared ashamedly at the floor. His sorrowful expression was enough to somewhat calm Eddie's mood.

"I'm sorry boy," Eddie said softly. "It's not your fault. It's just what a T-rex does, I suppose."

Poor Lainey, thought Eddie. Lainey never had much time for Eddie, as between her drama classes, clarinet recitals, swimming lessons and ballet practice there really wasn't much room for anything else, let alone an annoying little brother nearly three years her junior. Despite this, Eddie actually liked and respected his sister a great deal. He only really did mean things to her on occasion to get some sort of reaction. He now felt a burning in the pit of his stomach over what had happened.

"O.K, well there's nothing to be done about it now I suppose," Eddie told Bolan. "I'll just play dumb and pretend I know nothing and Mum and Dad will just think the poodle escaped somehow."

No sooner had Eddie uttered these words, when he once again heard the booming of thunder. His Dad was coming up the stairs!

"Quick Bolan, Dad's coming up. Get in the wardrobe and don't make a sound," Eddie ordered, shooing Bolan back into his seemingly ever smaller closet. Eddie locked the door behind him and dived onto his bed.

Dad rapped on the bedroom door and then clomped straight in. Eddie never understood why his Dad bothered knocking, as he never waited for an invitation to enter. As his Dad moved into the heart of the room, Eddie could clearly see that he still had a bee in his bonnet.

"Now, I'll ask you one last time son, do you know anything at all about this missing poodle?"

"No Dad, I don't. Honestly."

Dad studied Eddie keenly, before nodding his head. "O.K boy, I believe you."

Eddie sensed that his Dad was finally calming. "Right then, we've got a couple of hours before dinner, so I'm going to go out and look for this pup. I have a feeling he might be sniffing around Miss Dupp's house," said Eddie's Dad.

May Dupp was such a strange lady, that if you didn't see her with your own eyes, you would almost believe she wasn't real at all. May lived alone in a bombsite of a property. All manner of unusual items were strewn across her lawn. A bathtub containing hundreds, if not thousands, of old DVD cases, a rubber dingy and stack of tractor tyres were just a taster of the things that could be found in front of her house. As well as a variety of oddities, May also had a vast number of dogs. No one knew exactly how many dogs May had, as there seemed to be a different pack in the front yard each time you passed. However, she must have had at least twelve dogs and there would always be five or six roaming around the cluttered garden at any one time.

"Yeah, I'm sure the poodle has headed over there," stated Eddie's Dad. "He probably went over for a play date. Are you going to come and help me look for him?"

Before Eddie had a chance to respond, his Dad spotted something that totally distracted him from the upcoming poodle finding mission.

"What's that?

Is that?

Eddie.......is that what I think it is?"

Eddie's Dad edged slowly over to the corner of the room and bent down to inspect the item.

"It's a poo. A giant poo! Eddie, why is there a humungous poo in the corner of your room?"

Eddie had provided Bolan a litter tray and while he did use it on most occasions, today was

21

obviously not one of those days. However, being the expert liar that he was, Eddie found himself responding as fast as lightening.

"Jeepers Creepers! Lainey's poodle must have got in here and pooed in the corner, before it escaped. Don't worry Dad, I'll clean it up for you. That's the kind of son I am."

"Poodle poo? Eddie Smith, get over here and look at the size of this thing. There ain't no poodle on Earth doing something that big!"

Eddie hopped off his bed and bounded over to the corner of the room. Dad was right. The poo was almost as large as the poodle pup itself. Eddie knew instantly that his current explanation would not stick and he started to panic. Eddie searched his mind, desperately trying to conjure up an excuse to explain the situation. But, after some thought, he knew that there was really only one lie he could tell that would have any small chance of being believed. It really wasn't ideal, but there was no other choice.

"Sorry Dad, it was me," Eddie mumbled through gritted teeth.

"You? Why would you do a poo in the corner of your room for heaven's sake?" questioned his Dad, furiously shaking his head.

"I did it this morning and I forgot to clear it up before school. Lainey was in the shower and Mum was in the downstairs toilet, so there was nowhere to go. I'm sorry but I couldn't hold it, I've had a really bad tummy."

"Bad tummy! That's a bit of an understatement I'd say! Look at the size of this thing. It's colossal! How did *that* come out of *you*? And another thing, what have you been eating? It looks like there's cotton wool in there!"

Dad was right. The dropping was indeed entangled in fur. It reminded Eddie of the mouldy snickers bar that his Dad discovered under the passenger seat of his old banger when he hoovered it last summer. Only, this was several times the size.

"It was sore alright. I don't know what to say Dad. I've got a tummy bug, that's all. I'm sorry, it was an accident."

Eddie wanted this conversation to be over....NOW!

"I don't know where to start. I don't know whether to tell you off or take you to the doctor? That's not right son. That's not right at all."

"No Dad, I don't need the doctor. I'm fine again now. I actually went not long ago and it was normal again, so it was probably just a 24 hour thing. It's going around school. Justin had it too.

He managed to get to the toilet with only seconds to spare earlier and Claire Voyant said she could feel something coming on as well."

Eddie's Dad looked at him with a bemused look on his already normally dopey face. He shook his head and puffed out his cheeks in bewilderment.

"Well, I suppose there's no harm done but if that happens again you will have to go straight to see Dr Pepper. Right, clean that up and be downstairs in five minutes and we'll go and look for Laincy's poodle."

Dad was still shaking his head and muttering to himself as he plodded out of the room and made his way downstairs. Eddie let out an enormous sigh. Eddie loved Bolan dearly but being the owner of a young T-rex was hard, and it was getting harder by the day. When Bolan hatched he was no bigger than a small cat and as cute as a button, but now, ten months later, he was the size of a large golden retriever. Not only was it getting hard to squeeze him into the wardrobe, Bolan's appetite and energy levels were soaring and incidents such as this were increasing on a daily basis. Eddie decided there and then, that if he was to keep Bolan out of trouble, there was really only one thing he could do. Bolan would have to join him at school, where he could keep a much closer eye on him.

The Fool Proof Plan

After a pointless search for Lainey's poodle, Eddie returned home and began to plot exactly how Bolan could join him at St Nick's, without arousing suspicion. Now, Eddie wasn't stupid. He knew this would be a very hard task but after thirty-three seconds of serious thinking he had come up with as close to a fool proof plan as could be expected. Eddie remembered that around a year ago, Lainey's best friend, Ellie Fantears, had a foreign exchange student from France come to stay with her for a few weeks. Celeste followed Ellie wherever she went, which included attending her school. Eddie believed this to be the perfect cover for Bolan. Not only would it explain why a new pupil was suddenly and unexpectedly in class, but it would also account for why he didn't speak English.

Eddie raced over to his desk and brushed the mountain of sticky sweet wrappers off his laptop. He lifted the lid, opened the browser and typed 'Frenchman' into the images section of the search engine. Eddie had never been to France, so he really had no idea that the picture of a man in a blue and white striped top wearing a beret on his head and a string of onions around his neck, actually looked nothing like anyone living in France whatsoever.

Immediately, Eddie rose from his laptop and began to plan what he could use for Bolan's costume. His first port of call was Dad's wardrobe. Dad was born and raised in Brighton and since he was seven years old, he never missed a single one of their matches. He loved the Seagulls so much, that he owned every kit they played in for the past thirty years. Eddie knew that the blue and white hooped top would be perfect. He had to turn it inside out, so that the badges and logos were hidden, but once he did, it looked exactly like the jumper from the picture. It was a very tight fit on Bolan, as Eddie had to curl up his tail and tuck it in the back on the jersey. This made Bolan look like the hunchback of Notre Dame, which wasn't ideal. But at least the hunchback was French, thought Eddie. Besides, he didn't have much choice. Eddie could probably get away with a hunchbacked French friend but it would be harder to explain why his friend had a thick green tail! After squeezing Bolan into a pair of his own black tracksuit pants, the next item to be gathered was the beret that he was to wear on his head. Eddie had spotted many chewed up Frisbees in May Dupp's garden while he was 'looking' for Lainey's poodle, so plucking one through the broken wooden gate was an easy enough task. The string of onions proved trickier, as there was only one left in the fridge. However there were other fruit and vegetables available, so onto one of Dad's summer BBQ kebab skewers went the onion, a green pepper, a sorry looking carrot and two Granny Smiths. Eddie then attached some string to both ends of the skewer to form a necklace. To complete the disguise, Eddie slathered Bolan in Mum's foundation make up to cover his green skin with a more humanlike peach tone. As Eddie looked at Bolan up and down, he was rather proud of his work. Not perfect, he thought, but definitely passable.

The Fool Proof Plan in Action

Meep…Meep…Meep.

Eddie wearily opened his eyes to the worst noise in the world. It was the sound of the alarm clock alerting him to the fact that another dreary school morning had arrived. Normally Eddie would repeatedly hit the snooze button until Lainey entered the bathroom and he could take no more of her terrible singing in the shower. However, today was different. Today, Eddie leapt up from his bed like a jack in the box. His stomach was like a disturbed beehive, full of excitement and nerves.

"Come on Dinosnores," Eddie chuckled to himself, as he flung open the wardrobe door. Bolan wasn't laughing though. He was either too worried about his first day at school, or it may have been that he just didn't get it, being a dinosaur and all.

Eddie ran downstairs and grabbed a full box of Choco-pops, a litre of milk and a saucepan. After giving Bolan his breakfast, Eddie fetched the dust pan from the utility. He then put a quarter tube of toothpaste on the brush and gave Bolan's gnashers a good scrub. Eddie always used so much toothpaste to brush Bolan's teeth, that he had not brushed his own for months. Eddie got himself dressed into his uniform and fixed Bolan into his French costume. Eddie then sat him on the bed and flicked on Journey to the Center of the Earth, while he went to check if the coast was clear.

Lainey and Mum were always the first to leave the house, as Mum had to drive Lainey a few miles out of town to her secondary school. As Eddie entered the cluttered kitchen, he could see they were nearly ready. Mum was doing Lainey's hair, which was always a complicated task. Up, down, to the left, to the right, curled round and round. There were more instructions than the blooming Hokey Cokey.

"A plait, to the side please and can you make sure it's tight into my head this time, as Ellie has hers like that and it's fab," barked Lainey, as she devoured her final piece of toast, thickly coated in Marmite.

As Eddie's poor mother frantically tied Lainey's hair, she rattled through a checklist of things she needed to do before leaving the house. "Lunches are in the bags, Lainey's permission slip for her trip is signed and the car is defrosting. Right, I think we're ready. Come on Lainey, we're late," ordered Mum, grabbing her bag and keys. "Have a nice day at school love," she said to Eddie, ruffling his hair as she passed.

As the front door shut behind them, Eddie's attention turned to his Dad. Unfortunately, Dad didn't leave until after Eddie, but he was as regular as clockwork, so when Eddie reached the top of the stairs at half past eight he wasn't a bit surprised to see his Dad stride into the toilet with his new soccer magazine tucked firmly under his arm. Eddie knew that this was his chance to leave, as his Dad would be occupied for at least five minutes.

"Shut the door today Dad will you?" hollered Eddie, as his Dad entered the bathroom.

"Will do son," Dad replied, chuckling to himself.

Once his Dad had fully closed the bathroom door, Eddie bolted into his room.

"Come on boy, it's time to go!" said Eddie, as he hurried Bolan downstairs.

Normally Eddie would walk to school with Justin, but today he couldn't afford to wait for him.

Eddie took a deep breath. Then, he and Bolan left the house and walked down the path and onto the pavement. Eddie had worried that Bolan would make a dash for it once they were on the street, as he had never been out without a lead before, but he stuck to Eddie like metal on a magnet.

The pair strode purposefully down Rocky Road, before turning onto Goa Way, the short street that led to school. Eddie's nerves were building by the second, as they entered the school gates and walked across the playground to class.

Being much earlier than usual, Eddie had hoped that he and Bolan could slip in without being noticed. But his heart sank when he saw that Miss Taiken was already at her desk, supping coffee from her ridiculously oversized mug. As Eddie and Bolan made their way into the classroom, she stopped and peered over her red spectacles to view the comical pair.

"Morning Edward," said Miss Taiken, even though he was christened Eddie and not Edward. "And who may this be?"

"Err....um?" With all the effort sorting out the costume, Eddie had forgotten to think of a name for his fine French friend. "Um....this is Paul Pogba!" exclaimed Eddie, stating the name of his favourite French soccer player. "He's here on a foreign exchange from France."

"Oh really? Well no-body told me about this," fussed Miss Taiken, who was clearly taken aback. After a few seconds of furrowing her brow, Miss Taiken's face softened. She looked over at Bolan and broke into a horrible smile.

"Bonjour, Comment allez-vous?" she asked in a terrible French accent.

Bolan looked at her blankly and then he glanced sideways towards Eddie, hoping for some guidance.

"Quoi de neuf?"

Bolan kept staring.

Eddie watched the cheeks of Miss Taiken turn from pale peach to cherry red.

"Oh do excuse me," said Miss Taiken, who had begun frantically fanning her face, like a distressed penguin. "My French must be terrible, I haven't practiced in ages. I used to summer in Bordeaux with my family but that was years ago now, I must be very rusty. You probably have no idea what I am saying. My apologies Paul. Right, you better sit down then over there," she said, pointing to a chair at the back of the room.

Once the pair took their seats, Miss Taiken addressed the class. "Listen up class 4. We are going to begin the day with literacy. If you would like to get out your Word Wizard books and complete two pages by break time please and don't fret Paul, I have a spare copy here that you can use."

Eddie gazed over at Bolan, who looked hopelessly at the book Miss Taiken had just placed in front of him. Eddie slipped a pencil into Bolan's clawed hand and whispered to him, "Don't worry boy, just hold the pencil and look busy." Poor thing thought Eddie. Even if Bolan knew how to write, he wouldn't have been able to reach the page anyway. Eddie never could understand why a T-rex's arms were so short. They weren't designed for school work anyway. This became more apparent during the following P.E lesson, where Miss Taiken made the children play her favourite game. While she seemed disinterested most of the time in class, during dodgeball Miss Taiken stood keenly, like a meerkat, at the edge of the pitch. Every time a pupil got struck by a ball she would hop up and down in delight. If a child ever got hit in the face she leapt so high you would swear she was bouncing on a trampoline! Anyway, Bolan was hopeless. His tiny arms meant that he couldn't throw or catch a ball and he certainly couldn't use them to block. So Bolan spent a full hour being bombarded by a flurry of balls. Eddie felt terrible watching his friend being hit again and again. Bolan didn't understand. He just looked sad. When P.E finally finished, Eddie breathed a sigh of relief. Having Bolan with him at school had proven more stressful than he had imagined. But it was now lunch time, and a chance to relax for a while.

Lunch Time

Time flies when you are having fun. However, time must also fly when you are stressed out your mind, for despite the extremely challenging morning, Eddie couldn't quite believe that it was lunch time already.

"Right children, get out your lunches," Miss Taiken said, as she took a seat at her desk to correct the pupil's efforts from the morning's literacy lesson.

Eddie fished out Bolan's lunch from his sack and placed it down in front of him. "There you go boy," he said. "A ham sandwich, with extra ham."

Extra ham was right. Eddie had used eight slices! It surely wasn't what the Earl of Sandwich had in mind when he invented the thing. This monstrosity was a brick of pork encased by two measly wisps of bread, but then, that was the way Bolan liked it.

As always, the minute that the food was placed down in front of him, Bolan began gobbling it like a loon. Eddie noticed the hum of the classroom decrease in volume, until nothing could be heard at all. Nothing, expect Bolan's loud munching.

Eddie raised his head to witness his fellow pupils staring at Bolan. The pupils' eyes were bulging out of their heads in disbelief, as they watched Bolan's tongue flick out from his mouth to hoover up the final scraps of ham on the table.

"They all eat like this where Paul Pogba comes from," laughed Eddie nervously. "You should see him eat soup!"

As Bolan finished his sandwich and sat back upright, Eddie looked over to him. Bolan looked weird. His eyes were blinking, thick strands of gloopy salvia were dripping from his mouth and his nose was twitching like a bunny with a vicious flu. This was all too much for Bolan. The delicious smells that were filling the classroom were driving him wild. Chicken rolls, cheese and crackers, smoky bacon crisps. A Peperami!

"No, you have to stay sitting down!" commanded Eddie, as Bolan rose from his chair. But Bolan wasn't listening. He had now completely lost control of himself and his only thought was that of food.

"What are you doing?" said Mona Lott in her shrill whine, as Bolan reached her desk and scoffed her tuna wrap.

The very second that was gone, Bolan moved onto his next victim.

"Hey they're *my* cheese dunkers," bellowed Hugh Jidiot.

By now, all of the children were aware of what was happening and the classroom was descending into chaos. Every child was responding differently to Bolan's antics. Some of the prim girls were screaming and stamping their feet, some pupils were furious over their stolen food, some were crying and a smattering of boys were in stitches. One boy, Willie Holden, was actually laughing so hard that he had to firmly cross his legs to stop himself from wetting his pants.

Miss Taiken had seen enough. "What on earth is going on?" she foolishly asked. She could see as clear as day what was happening. "Paul Pogba, sit down immediately!"

Bolan wasn't paying attention. He continued to dart from desk to desk, gobbling up every morsel in front of him. Eddie stood helpless. Bolan was in a trance.

"Paul, this is your last chance. Asseyez-vous!"

Miss Taiken watched carefully, as Bolan moved back to his desk. Despite being cross, Miss Taiken also felt a little pleasure in the fact that her French utterance had made Paul Pogba sit down. However, it was clear to Eddie that the only reason Bolan had taken his seat was that there was no food left in the room for him to eat.

"That was ridiculous Paul," barked Miss Taiken. "Now, I'm not sure what happens in *your* school but here at St Nick's that behaviour is just not acceptable. At St Nick's you sit down and eat your lunch and your lunch alone. Now, as this is your first day, I am letting you off with a stern warning. But, should it happen again then the consequences will be much more severe. Do I make myself clear?"

With that, the bell went for break time.

Eddie left for the yard, gripping on to Bolan's arm for dear life and wondering what on Earth could go wrong next?

Thankfully playtime was largely uneventful, mostly due to the fact that Eddie stuck to Bolan like glue.

In the afternoon, Miss Taiken made the class watch a documentary about volcanos for geography. Bolan was so tired after the hectic morning that he fell asleep at his desk within minutes. He slept for a whole hour. Being sat at the back of the room helped him avoid Miss Taiken's gaze. But even if he was sat at the front of the class she wouldn't have noticed him slumbering anyway. She was too busy painting her nails behind a big book she was pretending to read at her desk.

Finally, the clock reached three, which signalled home time. Eddie and Bolan trudged slowly across the playground, wading through the sea of parents that were waiting to collect their little darlings.

"We'd better re-think this whole school idea my friend. That really didn't go so well," said Eddie to Bolan, who nodded his chunky head in agreement. "I actually think you're safer at home. You're probably even more likely to get noticed in school."

Little did Eddie know at the time, that it was already too late!

The Professor's Proposal

That evening, while Eddie was in his bedroom giving Bolan his dinner, there was a knock at the door. Eddie's Dad turned the sticky handle and yanked it open.

In front of him was a peculiar looking man. He had a mop of wild brown hair and a small pair of steel rimmed spectacles perched on his beak of a nose.

"Good evening Sir, how do you do? I'm Professor King but you may call me Lee," he said with a false smile plastered onto his face. "My daughter is Jo, from Eddie's class in school."

Eddie's Dad was immediately put on the back foot. It wasn't often that someone brainy and posh would arrive at the house.

"Oh yeah…um, I know you. Don't you work in that fancy lab in the city? You're a scientist or something aren't you?" quizzed Eddie's Dad.

"Yes, indeed I am," the Professor replied. "Listen, I'm sorry to disturb you my dear fellow but I felt that it was important that I come by. Now, I'm not quite sure how to broach this, so I suppose I'll get straight to the point. When I was collecting Jo from school earlier, I couldn't help but notice the little secret your son….."

Before he could finish his sentence, Eddie's Dad jumped straight in.

"What secret? What's the little terror been up to?"

"No Sir, you mistake me. Eddie's not done anything wrong," said Professor King. "It's actually not Eddie I'm concerned with. It's his......friend. You know, the one with him at school today. Now, I realise that it must be hard keeping all this quiet, so I have a proposition that I think would suit everybody. I would like to take the dinosaur off your hands, for a generous fee of course, and place it in the most wonderful zoo. There is a new zoo being built not far from here and once completed, it will be the finest in the whole world. There, the creature will have a huge paddock full of lush grass and trees and he will be provided with all the food he can eat. It truly is a top class establishment. Obviously I myself want nothing from all this, I only want the creature to be happy. On that you have my word. You can trust me."

Eddie's Dad looked at Professor King in sheer
disbelief, as if a tarantula was crawling across his
face. Suddenly, he began to chuckle, which
turned into a chortle and then into a full blown

guffaw. When his laughter eased, he managed to catch his breath and address the Professor.

"I'm sorry pal but I'm not sure what on Earth you are on about? You've probably been in that lab of yours too long. I reckon you've been drinking some of your own potions and it's made you go a bit goo-goo gag-gag," he said, still giggling to himself. "Listen matey, thanks for coming over but I think you'd better go home and have a lie down."

Professor King shook his head. "That is most disappointing. Look, if you happen to change your mind, then you know where to find me."

Now, Eddie had been standing near the top of the stairs, out of sight, during the whole conversation. But as his Dad shut the front door, he flew back into his bedroom to peer out of the window at Professor King heading home. This was huge. This could prove to be a fantastic solution to a growing problem. If Bolan could live in the zoo that the Professor described it would be perfect. Bolan would be happy and Eddie could visit him whenever he liked. Of course, Eddie wanted Bolan to stay with him forever, but he wasn't daft. He knew that in a few months it would be impossible to hide Bolan any longer. Yes, Professor King's offer seemed ideal. The only problem Eddie had was whether he could trust the Professor? He knew that he needed to find out the answer and that there was really only one way to go about it.

The Great Inscape

Justin arrived at the door, just as Eddie was about to leave by himself. He always had a habit of turning up at the last minute.

"Have a good day son!" shouted his Dad from the upstairs toilet. "Make sure you let me know if you make friends with any dinosaurs at school," he joked.

"O.K, will do Dad," Eddie replied. However, Eddie had no intention of going to school. He and Justin began the journey as normal, but as they reached Professor King's grand detached house, they stopped and scrabbled over the tall wooden fence that surrounded the property and ducked behind some of the thick, well maintained shrubbery in the garden.

"This is crazy," stammered Justin. "You know we're going to get in big trouble for this."

"Look, it's not every day I break into people's houses you know, but what other choice have we got? I need to know if I can trust this guy. I can't keep Bolan a secret for much longer. Do you know how big he'll be in a few months, let alone in a year? I'm already worried about what he's going to do around the house today after what happened with Lainey's poodle puppy. I just hope he stays out of trouble."

"Let's hope *we* stay out of trouble!" replied Justin.

"Relax, we won't get caught. The house will be empty all day. Jo will be at school, the Professor will be at the lab and Jo's Mum will be at work."

"Oh yeah, she's a pilot or something isn't she?" chirped Justin.

"No she's not," snorted Eddie. "Why do you think she's a pilot?"

"I thought Jo said that she works at the airport?"

"No, she doesn't work at the airport, she works at *Hairport*! That's the name of her hairdressing salon. She cuts my Mum's hair." stated Eddie.

The boys' conversation was then cut short, for the grand oak door to the King property opened and the sound of footsteps crackled onto the gravel driveway. Eddie and Justin peered through the gaps between the hedge branches to view the King family leaving the house.

"Have a nice day darling," said Professor King, kissing his daughter on the top of her head. His attention then turned to his wife. "I love you my snooky wooky bear," said the Professor in a daft baby voice, as he pressed his long nose into his wife's. Eddie looked at Justin and pretended to stick two fingers into his mouth to make himself sick. Even Justin, who was as nervous as a chicken at a fox's birthday party, afforded himself a smile at that one. However, the mood quickly became more serious, as the King's sleek, shiny automobiles left the driveway and accelerated down the road.

Immediately, Justin and Eddie tore open their school bags and took out the masks they had worn at Halloween. Justin's mask still had a faint whiff of sick on it, but it wasn't unbearable. The pair tested their walkie talkies, flicked their torches on and off to check they worked and were then set to go. Of course, they didn't actually need any of this 'spy' equipment, but it made them feel the part. Some survival programme had demonstrated to the boys that crawling on your belly makes you less likely to be spotted by enemies. It had looked cool on T.V, but Eddie and Justin had not mastered the technique of pulling themselves forward using their outstretched elbows and they just looked ridiculous. They looked more like two severely injured chickens than the secret service agents they imagined they were.

"This is harder than it looked on T.V," puffed Justin.

The pair had been crawling over the dew covered lawn for nearly three minutes but had only moved around a metre. Any small benefit they gained from concealing themselves on the floor was surely counteracted by the insanely long time it was taking them to scramble over the mucky grass. This was especially true considering that the tall wooden fence that enveloped the King residence meant that it was very private anyway.

After another few minutes of crawling, Eddie and Justin finally reached the edge of the lawn. They lifted themselves back up onto their feet and tiptoed over the gravel path that led down the side of the house and onto the back yard decking. Eddie's stomach turned as he inspected the rear face of the house. He had hoped that despite the cold weather, a window would be ajar that he could squeeze into, but it looked as though the place was closed tight.

"I'll have to smash a window to get in," huffed Eddie. I'll go look for a rock. You stay here and keep guard."

"Hang on, just wait one minute. I'll check under the doormat for a spare key first," said Justin.

"There's not going to be a key under the mat!" mocked Eddie. "Professor King is a total brain box. He's a deeply intelligent scientist who would never give burglars such easy access into….

"It's open!" interrupted Justin, as he turned the door handle, before returning the key to it's rightful home under the mat. "Let's be quick Eddie. I don't like this one bit."

The pair weren't exactly sure what they were looking for but they hoped they would know when they found it. The smart, all white kitchen shed no light on Professor King's character, only that he liked boiled eggs for breakfast and that he made a lot of crumbs with his soldiers. The wide hall coated with pristine wallpaper and the downstairs toilet also showed nothing of note, except that it was clear that Jo's Dad read more intellectual literature on the toilet than Eddie's did.

"There's nothing here," said Justin in frustration. "This is a total waste of time. Can we leave now?"

"No, not yet," pleaded Eddie. "There must be something here that'll help us."

No sooner had Eddie uttered these words when his eyes were drawn to the black leather briefcase that sat in plain view by the front door, next to the umbrella stand. "That's it!" said Eddie excitedly. "There must be some sort of document inside that'll tell us if the Professor is on the level or not." However, Eddie's heart sank as he picked up the Professor's briefcase. "Oh no, it's locked. You need a four digit code to open it. That's 9999 possibilities. It'll take us all day to find the right combination. It's hopeless."

Justin tore the briefcase from Eddie's grasp. "Come here, I'll try. I bet its 1234, that's the password I would use. You would never forget 1234."

"1234? It's not going to be 1234," snorted Eddie. "This is a total brain box we're talking about. The Professor is deeply intelligent scientist, who probably has very important documents in his briefcase. He would never have such an easy...."

"I'm in!" said Justin, as the lid popped open.

Justin emptied the contents of the briefcase onto the floor. The pair then removed their masks to get a better look at the pages upon pages that lay before them. They began scanning through the reams of paper that detailed the Professor's ideas and inventions, in the hope of finding some vital information.

"There's nothing useful here at all," sighed Eddie.

"Oh, I don't know about that?" said Justin. "Look at this one. Bread gloves! You put on a pair of gloves made of bread, grab some ham and a slice of cheese and when you slip the gloves off, you have a sandwich. I wouldn't mind some of those, they would save loads of time when you're making lunch."

"No Justin! I mean there's nothing useful about Bolan in here."

Eddie felt a sense of despair come over him. The thought of coming away empty handed had never crossed his mind. He needed to know if he could trust the Professor with the welfare of his dear friend. There was no way he would leave something like that to chance. Eddie felt a mixture of frustration and sadness welling up inside of him, but as this feeling rose up through him like water filling a bathtub, something made him stop very still. There was a muffled voice and a key fumbling in the door.

"Someone's coming. Quick, hide!"

Justin and Eddie flung the papers back in the briefcase, shut the lid and darted into the living room. They searched the space for somewhere to hide, with the only option being the long, flowery pink curtains by the bay window.

The Professor's Plan Revealed

Eddie and Justin stood like statues behind the dusty drapes, staring at each other in shock and fear.

"I'll arrive at the lab shortly and we can discuss it some more. I'm a bit late. I had to come home as I forgot my blinking briefcase. I've got too much on my mind with all this T-rex business."

Eddie's eyes bulged and he raised his eyebrows high, as he attempted to communicate with Justin through his facial expressions.

"Did you prepare the cage and order all the needles and relaxation drugs from the medical sector?" the Professor asked his colleague on the other end of the phone.

Needles and drugs? Eddie slowly mouthed to Justin, as if Justin had not heard. Well, Justin assumed that he mouthed needles and drugs. Eddie could have asked, do my knees look like bugs? Needles and drugs would definitely make more sense thought Justin, although he did glance down at Eddie's legs, just to be sure.

"That's great," stated Professor King. "I was thinking we could charge one hundred thousand pounds for each vial of blood we sell and we could probably fill two hundred vials each month. That's twenty million pounds. Two hundred and forty million in a year!"

As he continued his conversation, Professor King bent down and lifted his briefcase with his spare hand. "Don't worry Clive, it's for the greater good. You know how these things work. Thousands of animals are used in laboratories every day. We need to poke and prod them if we want to make scientific progress. Just think, this creature's DNA will create hundreds more dinosaurs for zoos and exhibitions around the world. If it makes us rich and famous as well, then that's a bonus," he said, breaking into a wicked grin. "It's win-win."

Eddie once again looked over to Justin. He looked strange. His face was all scrunched up. It reminded Eddie of how his Nan looked without her false teeth in. Justin suffered terribly with hay fever and allergies. It was a nightmare. From early May, all the way up until late September, he looked like Eddie's Mum after she had been watching one of her soppy romance films. His eyes were always red and puffy and his nose was always streaming. Unfortunately, the curtains that Justin now found himself behind were very dusty and this was aggravating his allergies terribly. As his nose began twitching, Eddie knew what was coming.

"Ah, ah, ah..."

Eddie was shaking his head at Justin, willing him to stop. But it was hopeless. Everyone knows you cannot stop a sneeze, no matter how hard you try.

"Ah-Choo."

Luckily, Justin had the sense to cover his nose with his sleeve, which stifled the noise. Eddie and Justin held their breath. Maybe the sneeze was quiet enough for Professor King not to have heard it. It certainly wasn't loud. Maybe, just maybe, they had gotten away with it. Everything was quiet and still for what seemed like an eternity, but the silence was soon broken.

"Change of plans Clive. We're not waiting until tomorrow. Send the vans over immediately, we're getting the beast today!"

Catch Us If You Can

"There's no way you're getting your rotten hands on *my* pet!"

Eddie had tried to sound heroic as he uttered these words, but instead he just looked foolish, as he clumsily emerged from the large curtains he had become tangled in.

"Eddie Smith! What may I ask are you doing in *my* house? This is breaking and entering, a very serious crime."

"Forget that. What about abduction and torture? That's what you're planning, you evil man!"

"It's an animal boy!" scoffed the Professor. "A fabulous animal, that we all thought was extinct, but an animal none the less. It's surely worth sacrificing one beast, to ensure the species thrives in the future?"

"No, it's not! I won't let you hurt my friend."

Professor King lowered his head. He peered over his spectacles and his steel blue eyes focused on Eddie. A sinister smile crept across his face, as he spoke softly and quietly, "You don't have much choice my boy. The vans will be here any minute to take him to the laboratory."

At once, Eddie began a charge for the door. He ran across the room and using the coffee table as a springboard, leapt as far as he could towards the exit. However, he was swept up in Professor King's long, gangly arms before his feet even touched the ground.

"Get off me! Let me go!" wailed Eddie. He wriggled and squirmed like a fish on a line in an attempt to get free, but Professor King was deceptively strong and his grip was tight. As Eddie continued to writhe around in the Professor's arms, Justin felt something in the pit of his stomach that he had never felt before. Whether it was rage, or courage, he wasn't sure, but whatever it was, it was having a huge effect on him and before he knew it, he was running directly at Professor King.

"Get off my friend, you big nerd!" he roared, as he flew towards the Professor. Justin was only a slip of a lad. Admittedly, he was average height, but he was as thin and as scrawny as a string bean. However, the sheer speed at which he collided with Professor King was enough to send him reeling backwards and the vice like grip that had entangled Eddie so tightly, relieved just enough for him to burst free.

"Run Eddie, I'll keep him occupied," commanded Justin.

Eddie dashed for the door, glancing back briefly to see Justin whirling his arms around, like a supersonic windmill.

"I'm a black belt in Taekwondo and you are about to have your butt kicked," threatened Justin. This was a complete lie. The only belt Justin had ever worn was the one he used to strap himself into the car. Eddie didn't have time to worry about Justin though. All of his focus was on reaching Bolan. He bolted out the door and up the driveway, before turning a sharp right towards home. Eddie wasn't a particularly fast runner, but with the goal of saving his friend in his mind, he was reaching speeds he never thought himself capable of. He could barely feel his feet touch the ground, as he hurtled down the street and through the open front gate of his house.

Eddie shoulder barged the front door open. "Bolan we have to go, NOW!" he shouted at the top of his voice.

Bolan instantly appeared at the top of the stairs, looking somewhat shocked to see Eddie return from school so early in the day.

"We have to go boy. There are bad men coming to get you. They'll be here any minute!"

As Bolan hurtled down the stairs, Eddie's walkie talkie began to crackle.

"Eddie, it's Justin here. I'm sorry but I couldn't stall the Professor for long. He's heading over to you right now, and he has a tranquiliser gun!"

Eddie shooed Bolan out of the front door. "You need to run as fast as you can boy," instructed Eddie, as the pair emerged into the front yard. Eddie knew that he wouldn't be able to keep up with Bolan on foot, so he hopped on his battered old BMX that was propped up against the wooden fence and pedalled onto the street. As Eddie thought about where he and Bolan were actually headed, a noise similar to a lawnmower began swelling in his ears. Eddie turned toward where the sound was coming from. There, at the corner of the street, he could see the Professor hurtling towards them.

Eddie glanced down at the Professor's feet and could see that he was wearing roller skates. But these were no ordinary skates! Attached to each boot was a motor and an exhaust pipe, shaped like a miniature French horn. A plume of dirty grey smoke trailed the Professor, as he rapidly approached.

"Going somewhere?" snarled the Professor.

Eddie could see the tranquiliser gun in the Professor's hand. He knew they had to move quickly.

"RUN BOLAN!" screamed Eddie.

Bolan shot off like lightening. As the dinosaur accelerated down the street, it took Eddie's most ferocious pedalling to keep on his tail. As the pair sped forward, Eddie glanced back over his shoulder to see the Professor readying himself to fire at Bolan.

"Duck boy!" Eddie shouted. Luckily, Bolan seemed to understand that this was an instruction, and not Eddie merely pointing out Donald Mallard, a local teen with large protruding lips, who was walking on the opposite side of the street. As Bolan and Eddie bowed their heads, a dart came whistling past them.

Theeeooow

"Turn left!" Eddie ordered, as he and Bolan twisted onto Penny Lane. As they ran, Eddie kept turning back to judge the Professor's proximity. Even though his roller skates were powerful, the Professor was still a fair distance from them. He was clearly finding it hard to balance properly, for he was as wobbly as a jelly in an earthquake. He looked like a new born deer trying to stand for the first time, as his knees twisted and buckled. Eddie then watched the Professor's legs gradually widen, until he was doing the most fantastic example of the splits he had ever seen. The Professor grimaced in pain as his bum grazed against the rough, gravel pavement. However, he somehow managed to return to an upright position and readied himself to fire another dart.

Theeeooow

The dart missed again. Eddie was glad that shooting a gun while concentrating on roller skating wasn't easy. Yet, he knew that all it would take is for one dart to make contact and it would be game over!

The Chase is On

By now, Eddie had formulated a plan. He knew that they needed to get to an area where the Professor would find it hard to manoeuvre his way through on his motorised roller skates. The town's main shopping center, standing on the perimeter of Black Gateaux Forest, was ideal. If they could get through the stores and boutiques and into the maze of trees, the Professor surely couldn't follow. However, getting there was the problem. While it wasn't far, the Professor was inching ever closer to the pair, as he gained in confidence on his skates. Eddie could hear the sound of the Professor's fierce exhausts growing louder, as they twisted and turned and dodged and swerved around the narrow streets of the town.

"Faster Bolan," pleaded Eddie. "He's catching up."

As they turned the corner onto Battered Place, the Professor released another dart from his gun.

Theeeooow

Again, the dart narrowly missed Bolan. However, Miss Teary, Eddie's busybody neighbour from across the road, wasn't as lucky. As he sped past, Eddie turned to see the old lady, cross eyed, with a dart lodged firmly in her forehead. Miss Teary dropped to the ground like a felled oak tree. Luckily, she landed on her shopping bags, which broke her fall. The down side was that her face smashed into the carton of eggs that she had bought only minutes earlier, turning her into a human omelette.

Finally, Bolan and Eddie reached Letsby Avenue. The tears were blurring Eddie's vision, as they rocketed down the long street that led to the entrance of the shopping center.

"Come on boy, keep going. We're nearly there!" Both Eddie and Bolan were tiring, but they knew they couldn't slow. Because the avenue was so straight, the Professor did not have to focus on turning, so he was picking up speed and gaining on them by the second.

Theeeooow

Another dart flew past. This one was so close that Eddie actually felt the air vibrate around him. The Professor was firing at a more rapid pace now, so Bolan and Eddie began weaving in and out of parked cars to shield themselves from the flurry of darts that cascaded toward them. Eddie could hear the darts pinging against the metal, as the shopping center came into in view.

Eddie knew that his bike wouldn't make it through the revolving entrance door of the shopping center, but he knew he didn't have time to slow down.

"Bolan, get ready for me to jump," instructed Eddie, as he raised his feet from the pedals and planted them onto the saddle of his BMX. They were just metres from the entrance when Eddie leapt from his bike and landed with a thud onto Bolan's sturdy back. Bolan hardly broke stride, as he flew through the revolving door and straight into the foyer. The Professor's entry was not as successful. He was travelling at such a speed upon entering the door, that instead of exiting as he should, he got caught in a spin. The revolving door began to turn faster and faster. It continued to speed up until Eddie could no longer see the Professor any more, just a whirl of colour, like a load in the spin cycle of a washing machine.

"Look Bolan, he's stuck," cheered Eddie, as the pair stopped for a moment to catch their breath. Suddenly, the Professor somehow managed to break free from the spinning door. However, he had built up so much momentum while in there, that he shot out into the shopping center like a dart from his own gun. The terrific speed at which the Professor was travelling meant that he was a mere blur as he entered Donna's Closest, Eddie's Mum's favourite clothes shop. As the Professor flew through the shop, he collided into shoppers, mannequins and tables of neatly stacked clothes, leaving a trail of destruction behind him. Professor King then jerked into the underwear section.

Eddie and Bolan watched in delight as the Professor clattered through a railing of ladies underwear items, emerging from the other end with a gigantic pair of pink spotty knickers stuck to his face.

"Help, I can't see!" the Professor yelled, as he desperately tried to wrestle the undergarments off. By the time he managed to tear the frilly pants from his face, it was already too late. The Professor smashed into the shop wall with a tremendous thud.

As he lay there on the floor, dazed and confused, a swarm of women ran over. They clamoured around him to see if he was injured.

"I'm fine, I'm fine. Get away from me!" roared the Professor, who sat up groggily. "Where are they? Did you see where the dinosaur went?"

The women began flapping like a flock of pigeons.

"Oh dear, he's seeing dinosaurs. I'll call an ambulance," said a portly women, reaching into her handbag for her phone.

"No, I don't need a doctor you silly old bat. I just need to find the T-rex!"

As the Professor attempted to rise to his feet, the gaggle of women held him down.

"No Sir, you must stay sitting down. You're clearly concussed," insisted the woman, who had begun dialing for help.

The crowd all nodded their heads in agreement. Each time the Professor tried to stand, he was held down by the concerned females. He was clearly no match for them and Eddie and Bolan could hear the Professor roaring a string of curse words, as they left the shopping center and headed toward the forest.

Into the Forest

"We're safe now boy. We can relax," said Eddie, as they arrived at the outer edge of Black Gateaux Forest. But Bolan wasn't listening. Instead, he continued to run into the forest. Onward and onward he sped. Deeper and deeper he went.

"Calm down, it's O.K!" shouted Eddie.

Bolan continued to ignore Eddie. He bounded on into the tangled web of trees, sniffing at the air like a bloodhound trailing a scent. As Bolan continued weaving through the wooden labyrinth, Eddie noticed the darkness swelling, as the forest canopy changed from thin foliage of leaves into a thick blanket that blocked out the shimmering, winter sunlight.

By now, Eddie was a great deal further into the forest than he, or probably anyone, had ever set foot before, when all of a sudden Bolan stopped.

Eddie looked around to view his surroundings. Bolan had led them into a peaceful glade. A small cave punctuated the tall trees and a pool of water lay flat and calm. Everything was silent, everything was still. Even the twittering of birds and the humming of crickets had vanished now.

Eddie hopped off Bolan's back. He closed his eyes and inhaled sharply, to get some clean forest air into his lungs after the most manic hour of his life. However, Bolan was not as keen to rest up. At once he set off again, splashing through the water towards the cave on the opposite side of the pool. It was as if Bolan was being controlled by an invisible force, as he lowered his head and hurtled into the cave.

"Bolan, wait!" screamed Eddie, who sprinted through the water to catch up with his friend.

As Eddie entered the foreboding mouth of the cave, he could hear Bolan making a strange barking sound up ahead. It was unlike anything he had heard from Bolan before. It sounded more dolphin than dinosaur. The light was fading rapidly, as Eddie moved further and further into the twisted rock. Eddie sucked in his stomach to round a particularly tight corner and that's when he saw something that had no right to be in a cave, deep in the middle of a huge forest!

Dickie Branston

In front of them, preventing them from moving any further, stood a thick metal disc. Bolan was barking like mad now and scratching at the circle with his clawed hand. Eddie ran his hand across the smooth shiny steel and wondered what on Earth was going on? Over the noise of Bolan's yelping, Eddie heard a laser-like sound above him. He gazed up to see a CCTV camera fixed onto the wall. The robotic eye moved, until it was firmly focused on Eddie and Bolan. The lens then narrowed as it carefully inspected the pair. Suddenly, the metal circle began to peel away, like the foil being torn from a tube of Pringles.

As the disc vanished into the rock, Eddie was greeted by a man, illuminated by a series of lights encased in the stony ceiling.

"Well, well, well. Who do we have here then?" spoke the man, who was only a little bigger than Eddie. He had kind eyes but Eddie didn't notice. His sole focus was on the thick, coarse facial hair that covered most of the man's face. The chap's beard was so large and bushy, it was as if a fox had leapt right onto his face, before curling up to hibernate.

"Oh my, what a handsome boy."

Although Eddie knew himself to be a total dreamboat, the man was clearly speaking to Bolan, for he was trying to peer around Eddie's back to catch a better glimpse of the dinosaur. Immediately, Eddie widened his stance to shield Bolan from his gaze.

"Oh, please don't worry," said the man reassuringly. "Your friend is perfectly safe.

Eddie could tell the man was smiling, even though he couldn't actually see his mouth at all. "Allow me to introduce myself, although I'm sure you recognise me anyway," continued the furry fellow. "I'm Dickie Branston."

Eddie looked at Dickie blankly.

"Dickie Branston? The famous entrepreneur?" Eddie shook his head.

"Hmm. Well, I suppose you are young and I have been off the radar for a while. Your parents will know who I am. I am the founder of the Virgil Company. I used to own a record company, a series of megastores and an airline, amongst other things. I was very famous and hugely successful in my day. A multi-billionaire in fact!"

"O…Kay," said Eddie, who was keeping a firm hold of the scruff of Bolan's neck.

Dickie could sense that Eddie was still nervous.

"Right, this will surely reassure you," he said.

Dickie pushed his fingers into his electric facial fuzz and let out a shrill whistle that bounced around the cave like a ping pong ball. Instantly, there began a pounding that grew louder and louder with every beat. Then suddenly, Eddie saw Bolan round the corner. Only it couldn't be Bolan, as Bolan was behind him. So if it wasn't Bolan, then it had to be…. ANOTHER T-REX!

Upon catching sight of the creature, Bolan tore himself from Eddie's grasp and hurtled forward. The two dinosaurs then began sniffing each other, drawing in large intakes of breath, as if smelling the most fragrant of roses. They then began chasing each other round in circles, each trying to nip the other's tail in a game of dinosaur tag.

"This is Mr Wagglesworth," said Dickie. "He is your friend's brother."

Eddie stood in shock, his mouth wide open.

Dickie continued, "Look, I think you better come in, don't you?"

The Beginning of the End

Eddie wouldn't have believed all this a year ago. However now, while still odd, it was just another chapter in the greatest story ever told. As Eddie sat in Dickie's magnificent kitchen, carved out of the thick limestone, he looked up through a glass porthole in the ceiling at Bolan and Mr Wagglesworth, who were leaping up to catch huge hunks of meat that one of Dickie's assistants tossed to them from a raised platform. "Don't worry, they're perfectly safe up there," assured Dickie. "There is a secure perimeter fence, so they cannot escape. Mr Wagglesworth spends most of his time up there. I purposely built the enclosure under the thickest part of the forest canopy, so that it couldn't be spotted by any planes flying over."

Eddie nodded his head. He slurped the last mouthful of coke from the can and checked his watch. He couldn't believe he had been sat talking with Dickie for nearly an hour now. There was a lot to talk about I guess, and they had barely scratched the surface.

"So how long have you been living here?" asked Eddie.

"I've lived here on and off for the past seven years," replied Dickie, "but I travel all over the place. Since I sold my business, I spend half my time in one of my secluded retreats and the other half going on adventures to strange and exotic places. That is how I discovered the eggs. I was on an expedition, aiming to become the first person to cross the Antarctic in a pair of flip flops, when I saw them floating through the water, encased in a block of ice. I couldn't believe the size of them, so I brought them home to add to my collection of weird and wonderful things that I've come across during my travels. However, during my trek from the edge of the forest to the house, Bolan's egg must have fallen out of my rucksack, as when I arrived back here there was only one in there. I retraced my steps a thousand times but I couldn't find it. Now I know why. I bet you were surprised when it hatched. I know I certainly was. To think, those eggs must have sat preserved in that block of ice for sixty-five million years until I came across them."

This was all so strange, Eddie's head was filled with a thousand questions.

"How did you build this place and keep it all a secret?"

"Money my dear boy! Like everything, it all comes down to money. I had the best architects and builders shipped in from all over the world to build this place. I paid them very handsomely for their fine work….and also their secrecy."

After a brief lull in the conversation, Dickie's eyes met Eddie's.

"Listen Eddie, I have a proposal for you. One that you should consider carefully, especially after today's events. I'm off again in a few days on my travels. I own a series of islands deep in the Pacific Ocean. I am planning to take Mr Wagglesworth to live on one of the islands. I cannot keep him here forever. He is getting bigger by the day and he needs to be free to run and hunt and live his life without the confines of walls and boundaries. I have an island in mind that he could live on happily. There are plenty of animals to eat, vast areas to roam and I would have my men regularly check in on him to ensure that he is content. Now, I understand that you would never want to part with Bolan, but if you want, I will take him too. He will be safe and happy with his brother, I assure you of that."

Tears began welling in Eddie's eyes. He had only just saved his friend and now he had to entertain the thought of losing him all over again. However, Eddie knew what he had to do. He had no other choice. "Can I come back and visit Bolan again before you set off?" said Eddie.

Dickie slowly shook his head. "I'm sorry Eddie, but no. If that Professor is after Bolan, he will have his eyes on you and your house right now. I cannot risk you being followed back here. What's more, you must never say anything about this place to anyone. I hope I can count on you about that?"

Eddie nodded his head. He understood.

"Look, I'm sorry to do this to you my dear boy but it is going to take you a while to get back home and it will be getting dark soon, so if you are going to leave Bolan, you are going to have to say goodbye now."

Eddie bobbed his head. This was all happening too fast and he could feel himself trembling with emotion. It was taking his every effort to stop the sadness from exploding out of him.

"Come on, I'll take you up," said Dickie, as he began winding up the spiral staircase that led to the enclosure.

As the fresh air hit his nostrils, Eddie knew that this was the moment that the great friendship was to end. He struggled out the words, "Come here boy."

Bolan turned and bounded over to his friend.

"I'm going now boy and you are staying here with your brother," said Eddie, choking back the tears. "Dickie is going to take you somewhere safe, somewhere you will be happy."

Bolan purred softly. He brushed his face against Eddie's and licked his cheek with his sandpaper tongue.

"I'll miss you," said Eddie, as he flung his arms around Bolan. "More than you'll ever know. You're the best friend I'll ever have."

"O.K boy, I'm going now. You stay here. You have a good life, you hear me?" said Eddie, as tears streaming down his face.

Gradually, Eddie released his arms from around Bolan's neck, "Go on then," he said. "Go and play with your brother."

Bolan stood staring at Eddie for a moment, before turning and running over to his awaiting sibling.

"I know it's hard, but you're doing the right thing," said Dickie, who put a strong hand on Eddie's trembling shoulder. "I'll let you know when he arrives safely and I'll send you videos and pictures from time to time."

Eddie smiled, as salty beads rolled down his cheeks and over his lips.

"Right, let's get you home. I'll have one of my assistants guide you out of the forest and escort you to your house.

As Eddie began the descent down the spiral staircase, he looked back at Bolan one last time. He tried to burn the image into his mind. One final mental picture of his best friend to hold in his memory forever.

The End of the End

It was nearly dark by the time Eddie finally reached home.

"Why does this door never shut properly?" growled Eddie in frustration, kicking the door shut. He ripped off his coat and flung it in the corner, before joining his family at the dining table.

"Tough day son?" asked his Dad.

Instantly, Eddie broke down. He sunk his head into his hands and began to cry uncontrollably.

"Oh no, has something happened to Bolan?" asked Lainey, worriedly.

Eddie's head shot up. "What? How?"

Lainey ignored him, instead demanding her own answer. "Is he alright? Please tell me he's O.K Eddie."

"Yes, he's fine, but.... how do you know about Bolan?"

The family all looked at each other and smiled.

"Oh come on now," said Eddies Mum, "as if a dinosaur could have lived in this house for nearly a year without us knowing. How many families do you know of that buy twenty sirloin steaks a week? Our butcher must nearly be a millionaire at this stage."

"Why did you never tell me that you knew about him?" asked Eddie.

Eddie's Mum smiled at him. "You did such a good job minding him and you became so responsible that we left you think that we didn't know about him, but we knew from very early on. We all helped look after him whenever you were out with Justin."

"And as well," added Dad, "listening to your terrible excuses to explain all the strange things that Bolan did around the house was hilarious. Watching you trying to explain that giant poo in your bedroom the other day was priceless. It took everything I had not to burst out laughing!" Eddie's Dad then moved closely into Eddie and whispered in his ear, "Mind you, once I finally realised what that white stuff in the poo was I wasn't as amused, but that's something that we'll keep to ourselves and never mention, alright son?"

Eddie nodded his head. He understood.

"So what happened to Bolan anyway?" flapped Lainey. "Did he go off to that zoo with the Professor?"

"No, he most certainly did not!" fumed Eddie. The family then sat in stunned silence as Eddie told them the whole story of the extra-ordinary day.

"I knew that Professor was dodgy," snarled Eddie's Dad. "Just wait 'til I get my hands on him. I'll knock his block off."

"You'll do no such thing Tom," Eddie's Mum replied.

"Yeah, there's no point Dad," agreed Eddie. "Bolan's safe with Dickie now and the Professor cannot hurt him."

The Smiths then sat quietly for a while. No one knew what to say, or how to even begin to process the crazy events that had taken place.

Finally, Eddie's Dad piped up. "I know, why don't we get a takeaway tonight from Mario Luigi's? For the first time in ages, we can actually eat the whole lot ourselves and not have to keep leftovers for Bolan. I'll grab the menu."

Being with his family, Eddie had begun to feel better. He knew that what had happened today was the best possible outcome for everyone. He would always treasure the times he had spent with Bolan and knew that their friendship was very special and while it hurt, he took great comfort in knowing that Bolan was safe and going to be happy."

"And look," continued Dad. "I know you don't want to think about this right now, but in a few weeks when everything has settled down, why don't we get a new family pet? A nice one, that isn't quite as high maintenance as Bolan."

Lainey's head shot up from the Mario Luigi's menu and her eyes widened to the size of saucers.

"Ooooh," she gasped. "Can we get a poodle?"

The End

Thanks for reading. I hope you enjoyed it.
No dinosaurs were harmed in the making of this
book.

37668199R00069

Printed in Poland
by Amazon Fulfillment
Poland Sp. z o.o., Wrocław